To Sue,

Major Payne in
HAPPY BOTTOM
Fowl Deeds and Feathers

Happy Reading!

Written by Heather Chamberlain
Illustrated by Robin Edmonds

Heather Chamb—

For June

Chapter in Verse

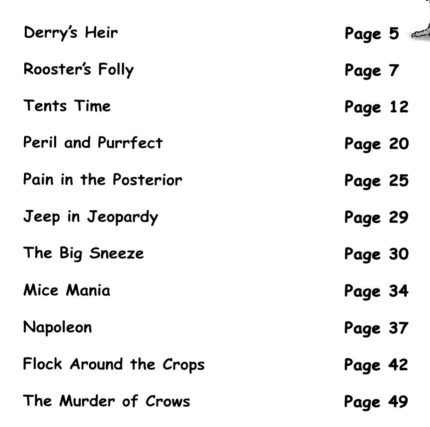

Derry's Heir

With curtains drawn the light was dim,
and Major Payne, now sleeping in,
saw dream turn nightmare in his head
when something jumped upon the bed!

The Major, in a bit of bother,
fending off the slimy slobber,
slid off the bed, then, clumsy clot,
stuck one foot in his chamber pot!

YUK!

The soggy sock could not stay on
and, once the icky thing was gone,
he grabbed his glasses from their case
and tried to see the creature's face.

Wide-eyed, peering across the room,
the Major saw, despite the gloom,
a hairy beast, though not a ghost,
who had, indeed, come with his post!

Woofbot frowned, was not impressed
when next his master (still not dressed)
said, with no thank you for his post,
"Wish you could bring up tea and toast."

In the mail there came a letter,
news of which could not be better:
Derry Ayre, who'd died in Tottom,
left Major Payne his Happy Bottom!

6

Rooster's Folly

In the morning sun, with paperwork done,
Major Payne had now claimed his estate.
So, at the double, crammed in his Bubble
he set off, unaware of his fate...

Along country roads, avoiding the toads,
he soon crossed the Piddle to Dimple.
Using maps on the day, he lost his way
(with satnav it would have been simple).

At noon in the square, he met with the Mayor
and Posh-Paws, his powder-puff poodle.
Woofbot took a shine, thought she was divine,
but they had no time to canoodle.

In The Piddle Pub, well known for its grub,
Major Payne, sitting down on a chair,
drank tea to unwind, then went off to find
Happy Bottom with help from the Mayor.

Stood at the gate of his country estate,
Major Payne to the Mayor then said,
"I don't care a sausage for this tumbledown cottage!"
And he walked away, shaking his head.

The Major went home; he wasn't alone
but nothing could make him feel jolly.
To him life was pants, till one day by chance
he met with a builder called Wally.

What Wally had said, the Major then read:
he designed and built houses for cheeps.
"Cheep" struck a chord — a house he could afford
would provide him with money for keeps.

The Major then thought: May not be his fault,
but this fool can't spell "cheap" for toffee.
Wally, though, was wise — he'd build a surprise.
And they struck a deal over coffee.

The Major's day came. The rain was a pain,
though he willingly trudged through the mud.
But what met his eyes — the clucking surprise —
had him speechless and boiling in blood!

"Rooster's Folly! Your cheep house," said Wally.
"For a cheep, as you know, is a chicken."
The Major felt duped — a right nincompoop —
and Wally would NOT be forgiven!

Tents Time

"You are dead," the Major said,
"if you dare to cock your leg."
He then called him a "mangy mutt".
Should be ashamed, tut-tut!

Woofbot fret, poor thing was wet
but wetter he would be,
if forced to venture in the rain
to wee against a tree.

Rain came in — it filled a tin.
Outside things went rusty.
 And everything inside the tent
  now smelled rather musty.

The Major frowned — he was so drowned,
his pants stuck to his bum
(the woolly ones he wore a lot,
hand-knitted by his mum).

Money spent, he loathed the tent,
(cursed "that wretched Folly")
and knew what he would like to say
to that birdbrain, Wally!

Then, one morning...

CAMPING
FOR
FUN

At first light and with the sight
of breakfast in a pan,
two shifty-looking men turned up
in an old Transit van.

These two scruffs, now living rough,
were conmen through and through,
who should have been sent on their way
and told what they could do!

Bogus brothers, Tim and Jim,
scoffed on egg and sausage.
Then said, as they sat slurping tea,
"We'll build you a cottage."

Deal agreed, they'd not proceed
till they'd been dished the dosh.
And paid in full they moved into
a hotel that was posh.

Major Payne then went by train
to stay with his friend, Arthur
(his Bottom left in dodgy hands
and destined for disaster).

When he came back to find a shack
bodged by a couple of chumps,
the bogus builders swiftly flew
with boot marks on their rumps!

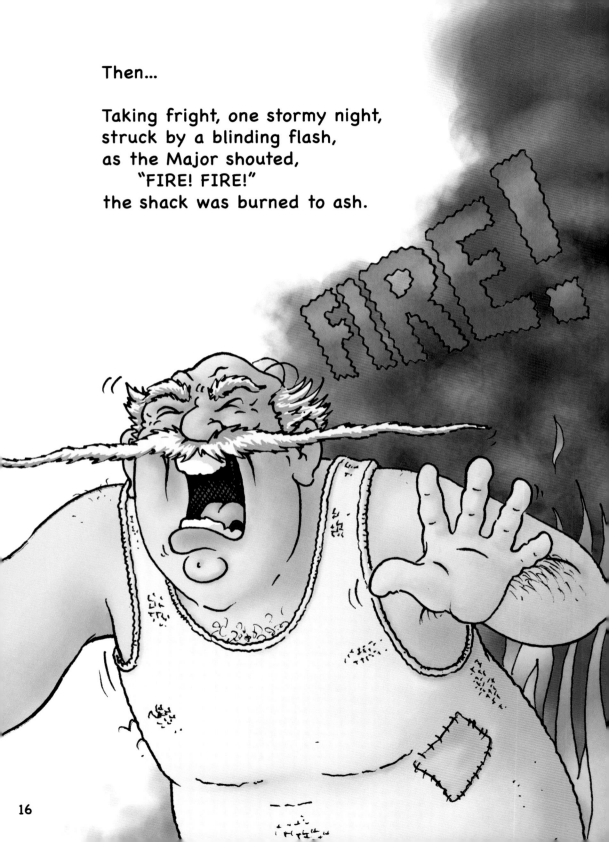

Then...

Taking fright, one stormy night,
struck by a blinding flash,
as the Major shouted,
    "FIRE! FIRE!"
the shack was burned to ash.

Back in the tent that he'd been lent,
the Major met Dan Goode,
who built a cottage, all to plan,
in Purbeck stone and wood.

So life moved on — the past was gone
(Wally, though, not forgotten).
And folk now passed the Major's way
to admire his blooming Bottom!

Peril and Purrfect

A cat and two mice travelled far,
stowing away in vans and cars.
But in a dark wood they now faced
the fear that they were being chased.

One mouse panicked; the other scurried.
Noses twitched; the cat looked worried.
They heard a roar! What could it be?
This was no time to wait and see.

Close on their scent but out of sight,
there raced a creature black as night.
The hound could kill them with its paws
and crush their bones up in its jaws.

The cat to mice said, "Hold on tight!"
Which they sure did with all their might.
She then turned tail — was swift to flee —
and scampered up the nearest tree.

With blood-red eyes and gnashing teeth,
the beast came prowling underneath
the bough where two mice and a cat
were now precariously sat.

The tree was rotten. What a curse!
But things soon got a whole lot worse
when trio, perched above the Piddle,
felt the branch snap in the middle...

They fought to keep themselves afloat
and, coughing water from their throats,
grabbed branches of a passing tree,
which saved the lives of two, not three.

Panic and cat were all aquiver.
Scurry'd been taken by the river.
Now dawned the fear he must have drowned,
been swept away and never found.

But on the bank a tearful lad
now told his somewhat doubtful dad
that a mouse had just hijacked his yacht —
left him with string and nicked the lot!

Scurry sailed to rejoin friends,
which was for all a happy end.
The yacht, meanwhile, stayed well afloat
whilst man and boy searched for the boat.

The river meandered (tree got stuck),
which proved to be a stroke of luck.
The cat and mice reached land at last.
Their Piddle peril had now passed.

Friends now continued with their quest:
to find a place not just to rest,
but somewhere they'd be safe to roam —
a happy place to call their home.

They found just that, thought it was nice:
a house for cat and barn for mice.
Made friends with hens from Rooster's Folly
but not the cock, by gum, by golly!

The cat was homed but at a price:
she'd have to spill the blood of mice.
For this she'd get her one desire —
a lazy life beside the fire.

Fireside, the cat, was now content
(was sure the Major's words weren't meant).
She dined on fish and played with mice
and thought she had the purrfect life!

Pain in the Posterior

The Major had a lousy night
when pesky flea found bum to bite.
He scratched the itch till it was sore —
said Woofbot was to blame, for sure!

His rump now bled, infection spread.
"You need a jab," his doctor said.
"Won't feel a thing. Lie on the bed."
Poor Major Payne was so misled.

At Pampered Pooch, when washed and scrubbed,
Woofbot farted in the tub.
Blamed for gassing poor Miss Fennel,
he was put out in a kennel.

"You're sleeping here," the Major said.
"Don't want a fleabag on the bed.
To think of what you've put me through,
in spite of all I've done for you."

Poor Woofbot sighed and closed his eye.
Without his master, he'd have died.
It came to mind how they first met,
the day he rushed him to the vet.

Woofbot had once lived in a flat
(not that he could remember that)
but fluffy puppy, kissed and fussed,
soon grew to be more kicked and cussed.

Abandoned, he became a stray,
where on a road, one fateful day,
the Major found him at death's door,
with one eye and a poorly paw.

Off life support, vet said he'd try
to replace paw and rebuild eye.
From injuries that were chronic,
came a dog who was bionic.

At Woofbot now the Major cussed
(his wound was worse and oozing pus).
To his house came Doctor Duttock,
jabbing more pain in his buttock!

The Doc when asked if he'd agree
the Major's bite was from a flea,
then said, "I think, from what I know,
the beastie was a mosquito!"

Jeep in Jeopardy

Now out of harm's way, punished, let's say,
and hidden beneath a tarpaulin,
a jeep with no pride was forced to hide
cos how it behaved was appalling.

One day in May, whilst taking away
a wall made of straw that was rotten,
the Major first peeped at an old jeep
that had for too long been forgotten.

The Major's surprise shone in his eyes:
this veteran machine, he was sure,
now sadly abused, had once been used
by the soldiers who'd fought in the war.

Jeep's story was not full of glory.
To the Major, though, this was unknown.
The question now: would he restore it
or conclude it was best left alone?

The Big Sneeze

AAH...AAAAH..

A sudden burst, by far the worst,
now echoed up the hall.
And in the kitchen icky goo
was sprayed upon the wall.

"Must be the dust," the Major cussed
(the wall wiped with his sleeve).
"But if it's that darned dog or cat
then they will have to leave."

An allergy to fur, perhaps,
more likely, though, a sign
that his Bottom needed dusting
and had done for some time.

...CHOOO!

AH — AAH — AAAH...
Woofbot was under the table,
Fireside out the door,
as the mega sneeze 'n' snot machine
caused carnage on the floor.

The Major phoned Bottom Cleaners,
none cheaper could he find,
which left him feeling quite content
till Wally was brought to mind.

The next day...

A woman turned up chewing gum
(which made the Major frown).
When asked if she'd come for the job,
she laughed and turned it down.

"I ain't come for no job," she said.
"I work for yer friend, Wally.
He said I should call round an' see
yer famous Rooster's Folly."

The Major scowled and Woofbot growled —
it was quite a shocker.
Then as he marched her to the door
someone knocked his knocker.

And there outside, dark-haired, blue-eyed,
stood whom he'd expected.
She smiled and after tea and cake
job offer was accepted.

Marie McGee was keen to clean.
Major Payne stopped wheezing.
The dust was gone; his life moved on —
free from snotty sneezing!

Mice Mania

Fireside is a curious cat
(not one for boots or fancy hats).
She loves the fire and has no vice,
except that she's best friends with mice.

The Major, though, was not impressed:
a cat that treated mice as guests
would exercise more pest control
if it found droppings in its bowl.

He'd found them in his muesli,
sugar, rice and loose-leaf tea.
Mice raided cupboards, causing waste,
aware that they would not be chased.

As matters went from bad to worse,
the Major cussed — his temper burst
the day a creature of such ilk
plopped right into his bowl of milk.

Scurry was in the porridge oats
(he couldn't swim and would have choked),
but fortune had him flung from doom
when catapulted by a spoon.

Panic whoopsied in the butter.
Through his teeth the Major muttered.
The escapade had caused alarm
but not a mouse had come to harm.

Fireside, now thrown out on her ear,
was told her future loud and clear:
"You'll not be welcome in this house
till you show me you've killed a mouse!"

Napoleon

Napoleon was a demon,
but no one knew quite why
he'd menace in his every mood
and evil in his eye.

The rooster wasn't one to trust
and Major Payne, not bluffing,
said that he would love the bird
roasted with some stuffing!

One day, well-armed with "shield" and "sword",
the Major took a stand.
But a swift ambush in his rear
soon scuppered what he'd planned.

With beak-scarred bum, his pants all torn,
    feeling mad, by golly,
        the Major swore to bag the brute
            and take it back to Wally.

Then in a skirmish one fine day,
launched from the Major's foot,
the flying cock, down chimney pot,
got covered up with soot.

The flustered bird then tumbled out
(feathers not so gleaming)
to terrify Marie McGee,
who'd been busy cleaning.

As black dust fell and she then fled,
Napoleon gave chase —
swift out the door and down the path
as if it were a race.

It may have looked a comic scene
but funny it was not.
The Major warned, "You mend your ways
or you are for the pot!"

Then along came Henrietta
to whom he lost his heart.
The cock was so polite to her,
she liked him from the start.

With charm turned on and temper gone
the couple looked so sweet.
Then one dark night, to his delight,
"I love you," she did tweet.

The very next day in the yard
(star-struck eyes on Hettie),
Napoleon sought cheep advice
from Old Mother Betty.

He popped the question. She said, "Yes!"
so love birds on cloud nine
invited friends to see them wed
and everything seemed fine.

Alas, poor Hettie fell unwell,
which made her quite moody.
Betty to Napoleon said,
"She's not ill, just broody.
Give her some time and she'll come round;
it's not you she's rejecting.
You should be proud — go tell the crowd:

Hettie is eggspecting!"

Henrietta the hen could not sleep.
At her eggs she kept taking a peep.
Napoleon yawned,
but, as the day dawned,
told the world they had chicks going cheep.

Flock Around the Crops

"Cockadoodledoo!"

"Darn that cock!" the Major said,
clumsily rolling out of bed.
He stubbed his toe, began to "dance"
in just his vest and baggy pants.

Arms up, then down, he touched his feet
(sometimes his knees — was prone to cheat).
"Last one," he puffed and, for such bother,
Woofbot praised him with some slobber.

The day was new and life felt grand
until he spied upon his land
a flock of birds, at which he swore,
"Stone the crows! We're now at WAR!"

The crafty fowl now scoffed his seed,
which to the Major was pure greed.
He shooed them off with sticks and stones,
but they came back when he went home.

"Arrrrgh!"

"Well, they'll not crow," the Major cried,
"when sold as dusters nationwide."
Woofbot muttered, "Bluff and bluster!
He'll not make a crow a duster."

43

The Major had to find a way
to keep those wretched birds at bay.
They came in sunshine, wind and rain
and were to him a major pain.

Radio on, he snoozed at last
till woken by a cannon's blast.
Tchaikovsky's 1812 on air
sent poor Marie into despair.

She dropped his trophy (it was cracked)
and feared the Major'd have her sacked.
But he then said, "Don't fret, my dear.
You've given me a grand idea."

What happened next was most bizarre,
the strangest saga yet by far.
The Major in a field, you see,
set speakers up beside a tree.

Marie loaned him some heavy rock,
a bit of jazz and funky pop.
With CD loaded, music on,
in just a trice the birds were gone.

The Major sighed — he'd won the war,
but such belief was premature:
crows that had just come a-flockin'
to the music were a-rockin'.

They partied on from dawn till dusk.
Their antics made the Major cuss.
And with their twitter, this fowl deed
was advertised to spread the greed.

This festival of feathered flight
was viewed by thousands day and night;
and those who travelled from afar
did so by van, bus, coach or car.

As social networks spread the news,
poor Major Payne grew more bemused.
Now in the press and on TV,
he wished the world would let him be.

With roads to Happy Bottom blocked,
it was high time the farce was stopped.
So the Major pulled the plug one day
and watched the chaos fade away.

But crows returned to flock round crops
long after all the rockin' stopped.
And posted warnings of their greed
were of no use when birds can't read!

Major Payne, with muddled mind,
now had a plan that seemed unkind.
He'd take revenge and, with a gun,
stake out the field and have some fun.

He told Marie the reason why
he'd "blast those 'dusters' from the sky!"
"That's cruel," she was compelled to say.
"I think I know a kinder way."

The Murder of Crows

As Major Payne tossed in his bed
there was one question in his head.
He could not sleep, just had to know —
how to defeat those wretched crows.

They taunted him. It drove him mad.
If they were dead, he'd not be sad.
They plagued his land, they were a curse
and there was only one "thing" worse!

Wide-eyed, he sat up. Tide had turned:
those crows would pay cos they'd not learned.
The land was his, all said and done,
so time now that he had some fun.

He'd blast the blighters, quell their racket,
sell their feathers, make a packet.
Win the fowl war trigger-happy,
live in peace and not be snappy.

Marie feared blood upon the field:
the fate of cocky crows looked sealed.
She thought it foul to fire at will
to see how many he could kill.

So are the crows now doomed to die?
Or will the Major now ask why
Marie thinks there's a kinder way,
and let her try to save the day?

Now that this tale is near its end
we're asking you to kindly send
a picture or a verse, let's say,
of how YOU'd scare those crows away.

Contact us @

www.happybottombooks.co.uk

On our website you can meet the characters and creators of Happy Bottom's wacky world.

In the scrapbook you will discover the real Happy Bottom!

We have included some activities and photos for your enjoyment.

Go to the gallery, where you will see a collection of children's work.

We look forward to hearing what you would do about Major Payne's murder of crows.

Rhymes and illustrations that you send us, whether they are related to Happy Bottom, or of your own creation, can be put on display in the gallery.

We hope you enjoy this book and that it inspires you to be creative!

One final thing before we go —

The answer to the question below may prove a useful fact to know:

Q What is the collective noun for a group of crows?

Major Payne in the
HAPPY BOTTOM
trilogy:
Fowl Deeds and Feathers
Mishaps and Mayhem
Peril and Promise

The moral rights of Heather Chamberlain to be identified as the author of this work and Robin Edmonds as the illustrator have been asserted in accordance with the Copyright Design and Patents Act 1988.

Revised edition published by Happy Bottom Books 2016.

ISBN: 978-0-9926091-0-8

Visit our website at:
www.happybottombooks.co.uk

Pre-production by Backtofrontdesign